This Little Tiger book belongs to:

_____

_____

_____

For Holly, with love ~ K W

To my beloved Grand-Maman.
Click, Clack, Croc' Geneviève! ~ J D

LITTLE TIGER PRESS
1 The Coda Centre, 189 Munster Road, London SW6 6AW
www.littletiger.co.uk

First published in Great Britain 2009
This edition published 2014 by Little Tiger Press, London
Text copyright © Kathryn White 2009
Illustrations copyright © Joëlle Dreidemy 2009
Kathryn White and Joëlle Dreidemy have asserted their rights
to be identified as the author and illustrator of this work under
the Copyright, Designs and Patents Act, 1988

Printed in China · LTP/1900/0816/1013

10 9 8 7 6 5 4 3 2 1

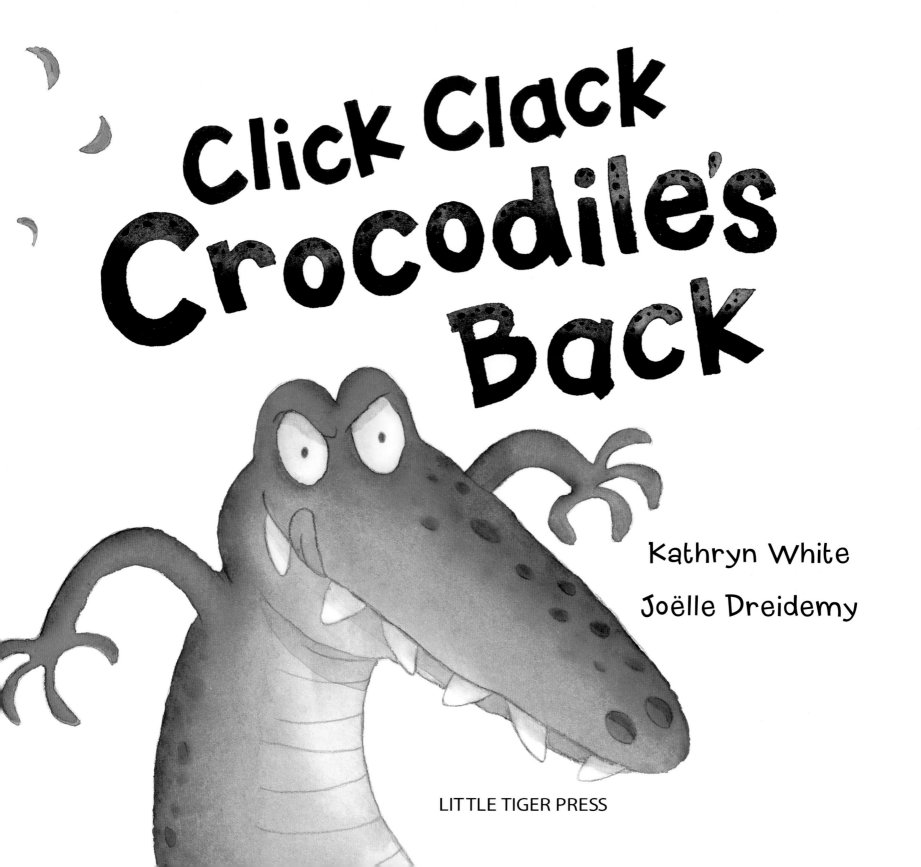

Click Clack Crocodile's Back

Kathryn White

Joëlle Dreidemy

LITTLE TIGER PRESS

Tremble with fear, Crocodile's near.
He's sneaking by, with a glint in his eye,
Slyly disguised as the trunk of a tree,
Ready to **snatch** you before you can **flee!**

Slip,
slap,
it's Crocodile's trap.
He's **squelching**
and **sliding**
in mud, where he's hiding . . .

Waiting to **snaffle** you
up in his claws
And **gobble** you down
with his terrible jaws!

WATCH OUT,
Crocodile's about!
Flamingos are **Preening**
then one of them spies,

Down in the rushes,
two **mean,**
greedy eyes . . .

"He keeps **creeping** up on me," Elephant groans. "That **big, sneaky** Crocodile," everyone moans.

But Monkey is cool,
Monkey is clever—
He has a plan they can
all do together.

So brave little Monkey swings down to the river.

"A gift for Crocodile," he says with a shiver.

"A **gift**?" says Crocodile, very unsure.
"Why . . . I've never been given a **gift** before."

Monkey holds out his **trembling** hand.
"This present will make you look
wonderfully grand.
It's a jacket I made from banana peel."

Crocodile grins
and says,
"Simply ideal!"

"We've made you a hat!" the flamingos flock in,
Making a **mess** and a terrible **din**.

And Crocodile roars,
"Oh, won't I look great?
I'll be **dashing** and **sporty**
and so **up-to-date!**"

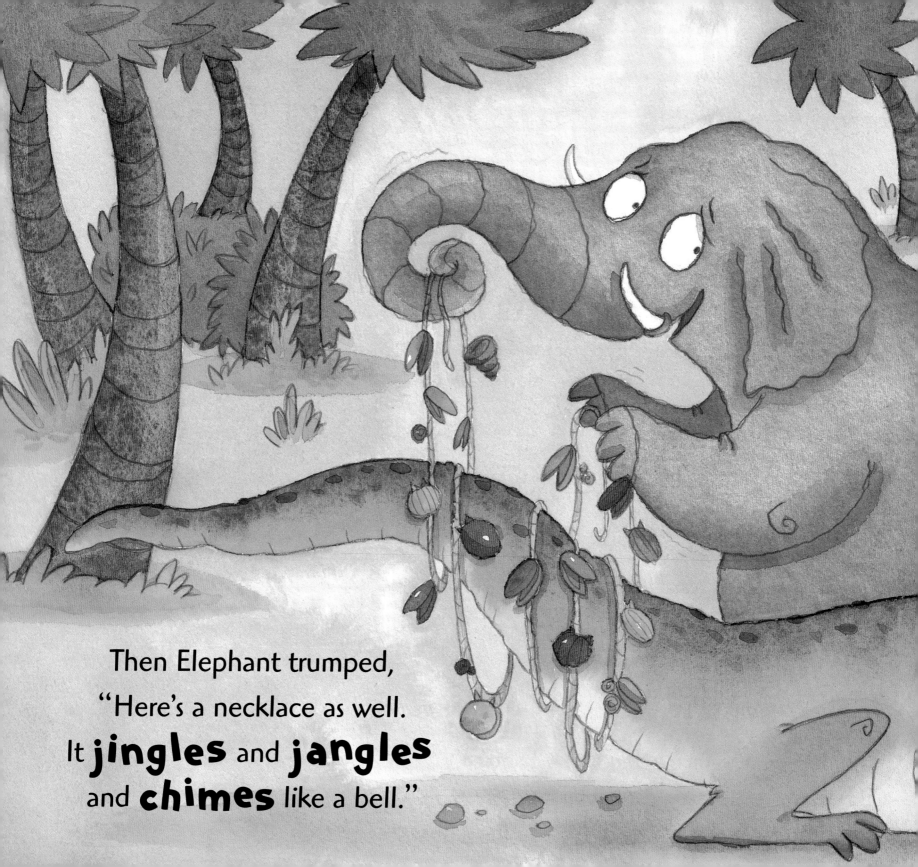

Then Elephant trumped,
"Here's a necklace as well.
It **jingles** and **jangles**
and **chimes** like a bell."

"OH, WOW,"
says Crocodile
with a big smile.
"Now I'll go **hunting**
in **fabulous** style!"

"And won't you
look **wonderful**,"
everyone cheers,

"When you wear these
new coconut charms
on your ears?"

"Awesome!" says Crocodile,
giving a

grrrowl,

"I'll wear them each time
I go out on the **prowl**."

So Crocodile grinned
and his **greedy** eyes shone,
As he shot off to try
all his new presents on.

Shhhhh!

Listen—what's making that sound?

It's **jingling** and **jangling** and **prowling** around.

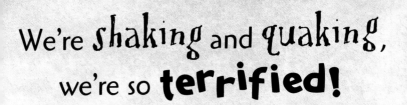

We're **shaking** and **quaking**,
we're so **terrified!**

It's a wild, crazy animal.
RUN FOR IT! HIDE!

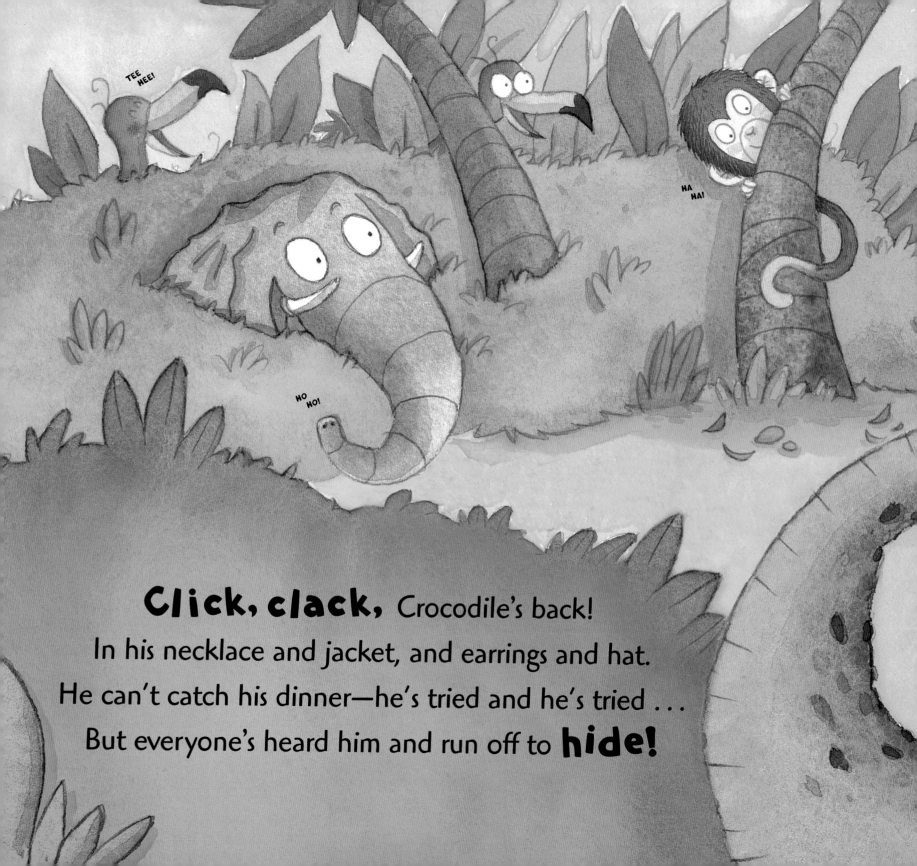

Click, clack, Crocodile's back!
In his necklace and jacket, and earrings and hat.
He can't catch his dinner—he's tried and he's tried . . .
But everyone's heard him and run off to **hide!**